Magic
Animal Friends

For Poppy Dare, with love

Special thanks to Valerie Wilding

ORCHARD BOOKS
Carmelite House
50 Victoria Embankment
London EC4Y 0DZ

First published in 2015 by Orchard Books

A CIP catalogue record for this book is available
from the British Library.

ISBN 978 1 40833 887 2

1 3 5 7 9 8 6 4 2

Printed in Great Britain

MIX
Paper from
responsible sources
FSC® C104740
www.fsc.org

The paper and board used in this book are made from wood
from responsible sources.

Orchard Books
An imprint of Hachette Children's Group
Part of The Watts Publishing Group Limited
An Hachette UK Company

Mia Floppyear's
Snowy Adventure

Daisy Meadows

ORCHARD

Shining House

Sunshine Meadow

Blossom Briar

Toadstool Cafe

Goldie's Grotto

Toadstool Glade

Mrs Taptree's Library

Friendship Tree

Maze

Silver Spring

Buttercup Grove

Lighthouse

Can you keep a secret? I thought you could!

Then I'll tell you about an enchanted wood.

It lies through the door in the old oak tree,

Let's go there now - just follow me!

We'll find adventure that never ends,

And meet the Magic Animal Friends!

Love
Goldie the Cat

Story One
Sugarplum

CHAPTER ONE

A Snowy Surprise

Lily Hart squealed in delight as her snowball splattered all over her best friend's knee.

"Good shot!" Jess Forester laughed. "Brr, now there's snow in my boot!"

Her tabby kitten, Pixie, bounded at her feet, springing up and down as her fluffy

 9

tummy touched the cold snow.

Lily patted another snowball between her mittens. "Oh, look!" she said, pointing. "The animals must want to play too!" The girls giggled at the sight of a dozen furry heads watching them curiously from inside a large barn.

In the barn was the Helping Paw Wildlife Hospital, which was run by Lily's parents. The pens outside were usually full of poorly animals, but they'd all been moved inside for the winter to keep the animals cosy and warm.

Mrs Hart popped her head round the barn door. "Lily! Jess!" she called. "When you've had enough fun out there, come and have fun in here, helping me check on the animals. Pixie can come, too!" she added, and disappeared back inside.

Lily and Jess adored animals and loved

helping in the hospital. Pixie dashed into the warm barn, but before the girls could follow, Jess noticed a trail of paw prints in the snow. "I wonder what animal made those?" she asked.

"They look like cat prints!" said Lily.

"But they're too big to be Pixie's," said Jess. "Could it be…"

The girls looked at each other. Both had the same thought.

"Goldie!" they said together.

"I hope so!" said Lily.

Goldie the cat was their magical friend. She lived in Friendship Forest, a secret

world where the animals lived in little cottages, and they could all talk! Goldie had taken Jess and Lily on many amazing adventures in the forest and they'd made lots of animal friends.

"Let's follow the footprints," said Lily.

After checking that Pixie was happily curled up in a nest of pillows inside the cosy barn, the girls dashed along the trail of prints. They led past a rabbit run, round the trees and behind the badgers' sett.

"It is her!" Jess cried.

There, beneath a fir tree, was Goldie.
Sparkling snowflakes glistened like
diamonds on her golden fur. She ran to
the girls and curled around their legs,
purring happily.

Jess and Lily kneeled to stroke Goldie.
She gazed at them with eyes as green as
holly leaves, then ran towards Brightley
Stream, at the bottom of the garden.

"She wants us to follow!" Lily said in delight. "She's taking us on another adventure!"

"Hooray!" cried Jess. "Back to Friendship Forest!"

They raced after Goldie, treading carefully on the icy stepping stones that crossed the stream.

The golden cat headed for a lifeless old tree in the middle of Brightley Meadow.

"The Friendship Tree!" Jess cried out in excitement.

Its bare branches were laden with snow. But, as Goldie ran up to the tree, it seemed to shiver, and suddenly all the snow fell to the ground. Glossy, evergreen leaves sprang from every twig, while bunches of berries and brown fir cones appeared on each branch. Robins and speckled thrushes twittered happily as they flew down to feast on the frosted red berries.

The girls grinned with
excitement as they read aloud
two words carved into the bark.
"Friendship Forest!"

Instantly, a door with a leaf-shaped
handle appeared in the tree's trunk.

Jess grasped Lily's hand as she opened
the door. Golden light spilled out, adding
a sparkle to the snow.

The girls followed Goldie into the
shimmering glow. They felt a tingle run
right through their bodies, and knew that
meant they were growing a little smaller.

As the golden light faded, Jess and Lily stared. They were in Friendship Forest, but instead of it being warm like it normally was, the trees and flowers were dusted with a beautiful sprinkling of snow. Everything glittered and twinkled in the wintry sunlight.

"It's magical!" Lily gasped.

"I'm glad you think so," said a familiar voice from behind them.

Lily and Jess turned and there stood Goldie, as tall as the girls' shoulders, wearing her sparkling golden scarf.

The three friends hugged each other.

"I'm so happy I can talk to you now you're in Friendship Forest," said Goldie.

"So are we!" said Lily. "It's lovely to be back. But why is there snow? It's always warm in Friendship Forest."

Goldie smiled. "Welcome to the Frost Festival," she said. "It's a wintry celebration that lasts for three days – and it's one of the few times of year that it snows in the forest."

"What happens during the Frost Festival?" Jess asked.

"Lots of wonderful things," said Goldie. Her green eyes sparkled. "Come and see!"

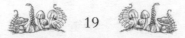

Jess and Lily followed Goldie through the
wintery forest to Toadstool Glade. The roofs
of all the pretty cottages were topped with
snow that glittered in the sunlight. And in
the clearing, lots of animals were playing
in the snow!

CHAPTER TWO

Tree Treats

"It's Jess and Lily!" the animals cried as they came rushing over to meet them.

"Hello!" Lily said, bending down to kiss Ellie Featherbill the duckling and Poppy Muddlepup the puppy.

Just then, a shower of tiny snowballs came from the upper branches of a tree.

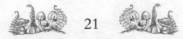

A cute little squirrel peered down at them, giggling happily.

"It's Sophie Flufftail," laughed Goldie. "Hey! Watch out, girls!"

They leapt aside as ten tiny sledges whizzed past, carrying their friend Molly Twinkletail the mouse and her nine brothers and sisters.

"Wheeeeeee!" the mice cried.

The three friends carried on to Toadstool Café,

where the
Longwhiskers
rabbit family
were serving hot honey drinks
from their café window.

"Hello," called a voice from the
clearing. The girls looked over to see a
little kitten building a snow cat.

"Amelia Sparklepaw!" said Lily. "Your
white fur's hard to spot in the snow!"

"Hi, girls! We made snow foxes!" called
Ruby and Rusty Fuzzybrush. The two fox
cubs were finishing the snow foxes with
acorns for eyes and pine branch tails.

"They're lovely!" Jess said. Then something caught her eye. She nudged Lily. "Look at the trees!" she said.

Tiny parcels, wrapped in sparkly leaves, dangled from the branches.

"Wow!" said Lily.

"They're tree treats," Goldie said with a smile. "Try some."

Jess picked a parcel and unwrapped it. "Mmm! Toasted pine nuts!"

Lily had hazelnut chips in hers. "Yummy," she said. "Who put them there?"

"You'll find out!" said Goldie. She led

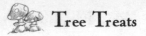

them out of Toadstool Glade to another

clearing, where sunlit snow sparkled

like jewels. In the middle were three ice

pedestals. They were smooth and perfectly

clear, like glass. A sparkling purple plum

rested on the first pedestal, and a huge

snowflake stood on the second. On the

last pedestal, a creamy white

snowdrop grew, its petals

tipped with silver.

"Ooh," Jess

breathed. "How

beautiful! But

what are they?"

Goldie smiled. "Those three things are the Winter Wonders. They appear on the first day of the Frost Festival."

"What are they for?" Jess asked.

"The sugarplum brings the treat parcels that hang from the trees," said Goldie. "The snowflake makes gifts appear outside the animals' homes, and the snowdrop brings the sprinkling of snow that makes the forest look so lovely. At the end of the three days, we have an extra special celebration, called the Winter Dance, and then the Wonders vanish until the next Frost Festival."

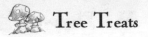

"Wow!" said Lily. "That's magical!"

Just then, a tiny figure danced into the clearing, spinning in the air and landing gracefully in front of the girls. It was a little honey-coloured rabbit, wearing a rose-pink tutu.

"Ta da!" she said.

"Wow!" Lily said. "What lovely dancing!"

"I'm Mia Floppyear," said the bunny. "Hi, Goldie!"

"Hello, Mia," said Goldie with a smile. "These are my friends Lily and Jess."

"I like your tutu," said Jess.

"Thanks." The bunny smiled. "That spin was the big finish for my ballet solo at the Winter Dance."

"It was wonderful!" said Lily.

"Thank you," Mia said. Her soft ears flopped over as she gave them a curtsey. "I'm so excited, I can hardly stand still!" Mia's paws didn't seem to stop moving. She spun on one leg, with the other held out behind her. "Are you going to the Winter Dance?" she asked.

Before they could reply, a yellow-green orb of light floated into the clearing.

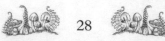

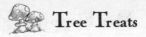

"Oh no!" said Goldie. "Grizelda!"

"Not again!" groaned Jess, clutching Lily's hand.

Grizelda was a bad witch who wanted to drive the animals away so she could have Friendship Forest all to herself. So far, the girls and Goldie had managed to stop her, but the witch was always thinking up nasty new plans.

"What's she up to now?" Lily muttered, then jumped as the orb exploded.

Cra-ack!

The witch appeared in a shower of smelly sparks, wearing her skinny black trousers and tunic. Her green hair whipped around her bony face as she stamped her high-heeled boots.

Mia trembled with fright and covered her eyes with her soft floppy ears.

Lily quickly scooped up the trembling little bunny and cuddled her.

"Haa!" Grizelda cackled. "The meddling girls and the troublesome cat! You think you'll stop me?"

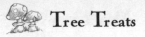

She shrieked with laughter. "Well, you can't! I've got three new servants, and we're going to turn your Frost Festival into a freezing witchy winter that lasts forever! No delicious parcels! No pretty little gifts! And lots and lots of snow! The animals will be so cold and hungry and miserable that they'll be desperate to leave, and the whole forest will finally be mine! Haa!"

She pointed a bony finger, shooting green sparks at the sugarplum, the snowflake and the snowdrop.

Cra-ack!

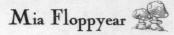

Jess looked at the empty pedestals and gasped. "The Winter Wonders!" she cried. "They've disappeared!"

CHAPTER THREE

Grizelda!

Immediately, all the treat parcels hanging from the trees disappeared in puffs of silver sparkles. The sky clouded over, and snow fell thick and fast.

Mia shivered in Lily's arms, hiding her face in her pink tutu. "What are we going to do?" she whimpered.

 33

Lily hugged the bunny tightly.

"Grizelda!" cried Goldie. "Bring back the Winter Wonders!"

"Won't!" the witch shrieked. "You can't bring them back, either. My new servants will make sure you never find them. Haa!" she screeched. "Friendship Forest will soon be mine!"

"We've stopped your wicked plans before, Grizelda!" Jess yelled. "And we will stop you again!"

But Grizelda just laughed. She snapped her fingers and vanished in a shower of stinky yellow sparks.

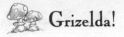
Mia popped her head out from
Lily's coat. "We can't let
that nasty old witch
spoil our forest,"
she said. "Or ruin
my ballet solo at
the Winter Dance.
I've been practicing
forever! We have to
stop her!"

"Mia's right," Goldie
said, "and there's only one way to do it.
We must find the Winter Wonders."

"Yay!" said Mia. "Where do we start?"

Jess, Lily and Goldie looked at each other in dismay.

"I don't have a clue," said Jess.

"Then that's where we should start," said Lily. "Looking for clues."

As they set off, the snow began falling harder than ever, covering every inch of the forest.

Goldie shivered. "The snowdrop usually just brings a sprinkling of snow, enough for everyone to have frosty fun," she said.

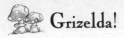

"But now it's gone, there's just too much snow!"

Mia popped her head out from Lily's coat. "I've got an idea," she said. "If you leap like ballet dancers, it'll be easier to walk through the snow!"

Jess and Lily giggled, and began jumping from snowbank to snowbank. "You're right, Mia!" Jess said, with a laugh. "Our feet don't get stuck if we dance through the snow!"

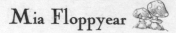

Up ahead, they saw a family of sheep and an old owl walking toward them, all pulling little wooden sledges.

"It's the Woollyhop family!" said Jess. "And Mr Cleverfeather!"

Grace Woollyhop the lamb pranced towards them. "We brought some magical hats and scarves to keep the animals warm," she said. "And Mr Cleverfeather has made hotpots!"

The owl's sledge was laden with little round clay pots full of glowing embers. "Sake tum," he said, getting his words muddled as usual. "I mean, take some."

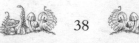

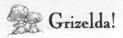

Mrs Woollyhop looked worried. "I've never felt the forest get so cold. Brr!"

She gave hats and scarves to Goldie and the girls, but Mia shook her head. "My fur keeps me toasty warm!" she told Mrs Woollyhop.

"Well, I'm pleased to have mine!" Lily wrapped a scarf around her neck.

"And thanks for the hotpots, Mr Cleverfeather," said Jess.

Grace skipped around the girls.

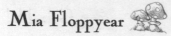

"Our magical
Woollyhop hats
and scarves never
get wet, however hard
it snows," she said.

"Wow!" said Lily. She took off her
mitten and touched the top of her hat.
Despite the falling snow, it was still dry
and warm!

Jess explained what had happened. But
no one had seen the Winter Wonders.

Just then, Captain Ace the stork flew
down and landed nearby. The snow went
right up to his knees.

 40

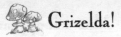

"Bad news," he said. "Harmony Hall is completely snowed in."

Mia's eyes filled with tears. "But that's where the Winter Dance is supposed to be held!"

"Don't worry, Mia," Goldie said. "We'll have sorted all this out by then."

"I remember Harmony Hall," said Jess. "It's a lovely outdoor theatre."

"Yes, we went there during our adventure with you, Grace," Lily said, hugging the little lamb.

Mr Woollyhop shivered. "It's so cold," he said. "We'd better go and find more

animals who need warming up."

"Ooh! Ooh! Do my hopping dance on the way," Mia told Mr Cleverfeather and the Woollyhops. "It will keep you warm. Copy me! Hop twice to the front, hop twice to the side, hop high in the air…"

The Woollyhops copied her carefully as they went on their way. Lily and Jess smiled as Mr Cleverfeather tried to dance as gracefully as Mia, flapping his wings to stop himself from tripping over.

The friends sheltered from the snow beneath a holly tree.

"We haven't found any clues so far," Jess

sighed. "I don't know what we should do."

"I'll fly over the forest and have a look around," said Captain Ace.

As he beat his wings and took off in a flurry of snowflakes, Mia gave an excited squeak. "Look!"

There were three sets of paw prints in the fresh snow.

"They have five toes and five claws," said Goldie, "so they're not from Mr Cleverfeather or the Woollyhops. Anyway, they're too big."

"Could it be Grizelda's new servants?" Lily wondered out loud.

 43

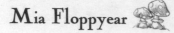

"Yes!" cried Jess. "Three sets of prints...
three servants... three Winter Wonders!
Let's see where they lead."

Lily scooped Mia up again, and they
followed the paw prints.

The trail led past a long, low wooden
building, its front door completely blocked
by a snowdrift. It was a pretty little
house surrounded by fir trees and a sign
hanging outside showed a drawing of two
pink ballet shoes.

"It's the Tippytoes Dance Studio!" Mia
cried. "I have ballet lessons here with
Wendy Inkwing. Put me down, Lily!"

She bounded towards the building.

The others followed. As they drew near,

Jess and Lily heard muffled voices.

 45

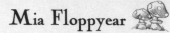

"Help!" the voices called. "Help!"

"Oh no!" said Goldie. "It sounds like there are animals trapped inside!"

CHAPTER FOUR

Wendy Inkwing

Lily and Jess found a window that was only partly blocked by snow. Through it they saw a beautiful black swan, surrounded by frightened little animals. "Please help us!" the swan called.

"We'll try!" Jess shouted.

"Girls," said Goldie, "do you remember

Silvia Whitewing, who helped us save Ellie Featherbill? Wendy is Silvia's cousin. Now it's our turn to help Wendy!"

"But how?" wondered Lily. "The snow's too deep and we haven't got anything to dig with."

Jess grinned. "We have these," she said, holding out the hotpot Mr Cleverfeather had given her. "If we put them all together, we can melt a path to the door!"

They put all four hotpots as close to the door as possible. As the snow melted, they pushed the hotpots forward. Soon, they'd cleared enough snow to be able to dig

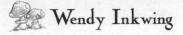

away the last of it with their hands.

Lily dragged the door open.

There was a great cheer from inside.
"Thank you, girls!" Wendy said, rushing
out and spreading her wings to hug them.
"And Goldie and Mia, too!"

Her class appeared, all carrying
ballet shoes, some wearing headbands
and legwarmers. Wendy pulled a long
neckwarmer over her head and gave all
the little animals scarves and hats.

"We thought we'd be stuck in there forever," cried Olivia Nibblesqueak the hamster, running to hug the girls.

"It's strange," said Wendy. "I know a magical dance that makes snow melt – the Snow-Away Dance! So we did it, didn't we, class?"

They all nodded.

"But it didn't work," said Emily Prickleback the hedgehog.

"We tried really hard," said Chloe Slipperslide the otter.

"I'm sure you did," said Jess, stroking Chloe's soft cheek.

"It would be so much easier to look for the Winter Wonders without all this snow," Lily said. "The Snow-Away Dance could be just what we need! Maybe we should try it again."

"The Snow-Away Dance hasn't been used for years," Wendy explained. "My grandmother taught it to me – Friendship Forest was much snowier when she was young. This is the first time I've danced it since then. I'm sure I've remembered the instructions properly, but nothing happened when we tried it!"

"Show us the dance," Lily suggested.

"If we all do it, maybe the magic will work this time."

"All right," said Wendy. "Listen and copy me. First dance in a circle around and around…"

Everyone skipped around in their own tiny circle.

"Reach to the sky and reach to the ground," Wendy continued.

They stretched up, then down.

"Clap your paws together, up high and down low…"

They clapped up in the air, then down by their knees.

"Now you will see the cold snow GO!"

Everyone looked around expectantly.

"Nothing's happening," Jess said.

"I don't understand," said Wendy. "I'm sure those words are right."

Lily smoothed the swan's soft black wing. "Never mind," she said.

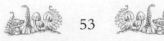

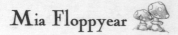

"Where did all this snow come from?" asked Wendy.

Jess explained about the missing Winter Wonders. "Lily, Goldie and I will find them somehow," she promised.

"Me, too!" said Mia. She hopped lightly backwards and forwards, making dotty paw patterns in the snow.

"Good luck!" called Wendy. "Come on, little ones!" The black swan started to lead all her pupils home.

"We'd better carry on following those pawprints," said Lily. She gave a worried frown. "But if it keeps snowing so hard,

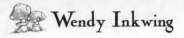

they will soon disappear."

Jess grabbed her arm. "I don't think that matters," she said. "Listen! Voices! Someone's just ahead, in that clearing."

Keeping out of sight, they peered through the trees.

In the middle of the clearing stood three fluffy white bears, putting the finishing touches to an ice igloo! They were as big as Goldie, and had shiny black noses and big, twinkly eyes.

"Now we know who made the paw prints," whispered Lily. "Bears! They look so sweet!"

"They do," agreed Jess, "but I think they must be Grizelda's servants!"

"How do you know?" asked Goldie.

Jess pointed.

One of the bears was holding something in its paws – a sparkling violet plum.

Lily gasped. "It's one of the Winter Wonders!"

CHAPTER FIVE

Sleepy Bears

"We must get the sugarplum back!" said Jess. "But how do we get it from those bears? And where could the other Winter Wonders be?"

"Maybe they're in that igloo," said Lily. "Let's wait and see." She crouched down with Mia, Goldie and Jess.

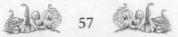

"I love the forest now there's lots of snow!" exclaimed the first bear, who was wearing a pair of purple earmuffs. "Catch, Minty!" she threw the sugarplum to one of the others, who was wearing a red bobble hat.

"Me too, Pearl," Minty replied as he caught it. "How about you, Sleet?"

The third bear tied his blue scarf and yawned. "Yes, it's nearly as snowy as our home on Snowcap Mountain," he said.

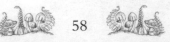

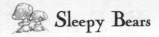

"It'll soon be just like Grizelda wants!"

"Aren't we clever?" Minty said. "Now
that we've got the
Winter Wonders
safe in our igloo, the
forest will stay like this
forever!"

"The Winter Wonders
are in the igloo!" Lily
whispered to the others.

Pearl yawned and set
the sugarplum on top of the igloo. "All
that playing has tired me out," she said.
"Let's have a nap."

Jess turned to Lily, Goldie and Mia, and grinned. "If they fall asleep, we can grab the Winter Wonders," she whispered.

But instead, Minty scooped up a pawful of snow and threw it at Sleet.

Sleet shrieked and giggled. "Snowballs!" he cried. "Come on! Let's get Pearl!"

Lily groaned. "They're not sleepy any more," she said quietly. "Let's move where they can't hear us, so we can talk about what to do."

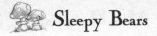

Once they were sheltering beneath a fir tree, Jess said, "Minty's given me an idea. The bears seem to like playing, don't they? Well, if we start a snowball fight, one of us can run and get the sugarplum while they're distracted. And we can look inside the igloo for all the other Winter Wonders, too."

"Great!" said Lily. "Let's give it a try."

They made lots of snowballs and stacked them at the edge of the clearing.

"Whoever goes to get the Winter Wonders must be careful not to be seen," said Jess. "If the bears guess what we're

planning, they'll take the Wonders and
hide them somewhere else."

"My dancing paws are lightning
fast!" said Mia, hopping up and down.
"I'll do it!"

Jess dropped a kiss between the little
bunny's soft ears. "Thanks, Mia. We're
ready! Come on, let's play!"

Jess scooped up a snowball
and lobbed it at the
bears. It splattered
right in the middle
of Pearl's white,
furry belly.

"Hey!" Pearl cried. "Who did that?"

The three bears looked around and
spotted Goldie, Mia and the girls.

"Another snowball fight!" cried Minty
with a grin. He gathered up snow with his
paws and tossed it at Lily.

Thuummmp! The snowball hit her
shoulder.

Splat! "Ooh! That's
cold!" Lily said.

The three bears
all shrieked and
shouted with
laughter.

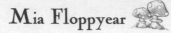

Soon the air was filled with flying snowballs!

Jess tossed a snowball at a giggling Sleet, then turned to Mia. "OK, now!" she whispered. "While the bears aren't looking!"

Mia nodded, and hopped gracefully to the igloo, twirling to avoid the snowballs.

Minty the bear threw a snowball at Goldie, then glanced at the sugarplum on top of the igloo.

Oh no, thought Jess. *He's going to see Mia if we don't do something!*

Jess grabbed another snowball and

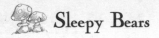

aimed at Minty's red hat. "Hey!" she
yelled. "Over here!"

Minty looked round just as Jess threw the
snowball. It splattered on the little bear's
head, and he yelped with glee as his hat
went spinning off across the snow.

"Look," said Lily, "Mia's almost there!"

Jess and Lily held their breath as the
little bunny climbed to the top
of the igloo and grabbed the
sugarplum.

"She's done it!"
cried Goldie, as
Mia slid down.

"Now she just has to look inside the igloo for the other Wonders!"

But as Mia crept towards the igloo doorway, the bears started to yawn again. Pearl dropped the snowball she was holding and was holding and stretched.

"Sleepy time," said Sleet, and the three bears turned towards the igloo.

Lily drew a sharp breath. "Oh no! They will see Mia!"

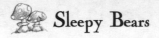

But the little bunny quickly twirled and leaped behind a snowbank.

"Phew! She's safe," Jess said as the bears went inside the igloo.

Mia scampered back to lots of happy hugs and kisses. "Sorry I couldn't look for the other Wonders," she said, shaking snow from her tutu.

"You did wonderfully," said Jess. "We've got the sugarplum now, and we can look for the other Wonders tomorrow. It's getting late!"

They hurried through the snow, back to the three ice pedestals.

Mia placed the sugarplum on the pedestal, and the girls gazed in delight as it twinkled with magical light. Instantly, little parcels appeared again on the trees. Cheers and excited squeals echoed from animals all over the forest.

Mia led Goldie and the girls in a dance of joy. As they hopped and skipped after her, Lily, Jess and Goldie each picked a little parcel.

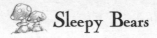

Finally they stopped to eat their treats.

"I didn't realise I was so hungry," said
Jess, enjoying some chestnut nuggets.
"Snowball fights are hungry work!"

Goldie nodded. "We'd better go back to
the igloo tomorrow and work out a way
to get the snowflake and the snowdrop,"
she said. "The forest will be completely
snowed under if we don't."

"And we won't be able to
have the Winter Dance,"
added Mia sadly.

"I've practised so hard! My family are looking forward to watching me. I've just *got* to do my dance."

Jess hugged her. "We'll make sure you do," she promised. "We've got one Winter Wonder. And we'll get the other two back – somehow!"

Story Two
Snowflake

CHAPTER ONE

Mia's News

Jess woke up snuggled in a nest of warm blankets and quilts.

"Where am I?" she wondered.

Then she remembered. She and Lily had stayed overnight in Goldie's Grotto. It was a cosy, comfortable cave with a red front door and a soft, mossy floor. Goldie was in

bed, purring in her sleep. For a moment,
Jess thought her parents would be worried
about her, but then she remembered
that time stood still when they were in
Friendship Forest. No one would ever
know they'd been away.

Beside Jess, Lily stirred and sat up with
a big stretch. "Morning, Lily! Morning,
Goldie!" she said.

The beautiful cat opened her eyes.
"I dreamed someone stole the sugarplum
and baked it in a pie," she said.

Jess giggled, then peeked through the
window. "The sugarplum must be safe," she

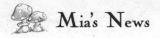

said. "There are still parcels hanging from the tree branches. But now we have to go back to the igloo and get the two other Winter Wonders."

Goldie bounded out of bed. "Breakfast first! Hot chocolate and toasted banana sandwiches?"

"Mmm, yes please!" Lily and Jess cried.

They ate their breakfast and were just finishing their hot chocolate when there was a knock at the door and they heard Mia's voice.

"Let me in!" she cried. "It's important."

Jess opened the door, and Mia tumbled in together with a little avalanche of snow.

"Goodness, it's deep," said Lily, as Jess brushed snow from the bunny's fur and wrapped her in a warm blanket.

Mia was so excited she couldn't stop twirling. "Dad went to the Nibblesqueak Bakery to buy carrot bread," she said, "and when he passed the Wide Lake, he saw the

three white bears. And one of them was
carrying the snowflake!"

Goldie and the girls looked at
each other in delight.

"Clever bunny!" said Lily,
planting a kiss on Mia's
woffly nose. "Then
we're off to the
Wide Lake!"

She tucked
Mia inside her coat, and giggled as the
rabbit's floppy ears tickled her face.

Once everyone else was wrapped up
in magical scarves and hats, they set off,

trudging through heavily falling snow.
Everywhere was quiet, with hardly an
animal to be seen.

As they reached the Wide Lake's
sandy shore, they gasped. The lake was
completely frozen!

"Friendship Forest has never been this
cold before—" Goldie began, then her ears
pricked up.

"Woo-hooo!" they heard.

There were more excited
yells and shouts.

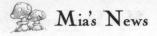

Peering through the falling snowflakes, Jess and Lily spotted the bears, out on the ice!

Minty cupped his paws round his mouth and shouted, "One…two…three…"

"Wheeee!" the bears yelled as they dived onto the ice and slid across it on their tummies!

Pearl laughed. "Now that we've hidden the snowflake, we can play all day!"

Lily groaned. "Oh no!"

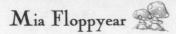

"It sounds like they've only just hidden the snowflake," said Goldie, "so it must be nearby."

"Maybe it's out on the ice somewhere?" Jess thought out loud.

As the bears disappeared into the trees, Goldie and the girls walked to the edge of the frozen lake. Mia hopped past them.

"This ice will be great for practising pirouettes," said the little bunny. "I've been trying to spin on my toes, and I must be perfect for the Winter Dance."

"Mia, wait!" Goldie called out. "Don't go on the ice, we don't know if it's safe!"

But Mia was already twirling out onto the lake. She spun round and round, faster and faster, then landed on all fours with her fluffy white tail in the air.

"Ooooh!" she wailed. "It's so slippery!"

She tried to get up, but her tiny paws slid on the ice and she landed on her tummy.

"We're coming!" cried Jess. But as soon as she and Lily stepped onto the ice,

 81

their feet slid too, and they fell onto their

bottoms with a bump!

"What are we going to do?" said Lily,

struggling to stand up. "If we can't cross

the ice, how are we ever going to find the

snowflake?"

CHAPTER TWO

A Rescue

As the girls looked at the little bunny slipping and sliding on the ice, there was a sound from the forest.

"Listen," said Jess. "Someone's coming!"

A group of young animals – kittens, hamsters, a vole and a badger – were walking through the trees towards the lake.

They were followed by Mr Cleverfeather the owl, who was pulling a sledge piled high with ice skates. Two robins were perched on top of the sledge, singing merrily.

"Hello!" the girls shouted.

"Hello, Liss and Jelly!" the owl called. "I mean, Jess and Lily! Since the weather is so cold, we're making the best of it by laking on the skate – I mean skating on the lake.

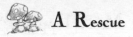

And Mary and Eve Redbreast the robins want to play ice hockey," he said, "so they've brought hockey sticks."

While the Redbreasts unpacked their bag, Mr Cleverfeather spoke quietly to the girls. "You look worried. Rots wong? I mean, what's wrong?"

"Mia's stuck out there, and we can't get to her," Jess said, pointing. "Could the animals skate out and rescue her?"

"Of course," said Mr Cleverfeather. He called the little animals and handed out skates. Then he gave some to Goldie and the girls, too. "You three can go with them and help."

Lily and Jess stared at the tiny skates.

"They're too small," Jess whispered. "And they're made for animal paws, not girls' feet! They'll never fit."

Goldie smiled. "They will. Watch me."

As she put her skates on, they grew to fit her paws perfectly. Then Percy Littlepaw the vole put some on his tiny paws. They fitted perfectly, too!

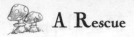

Jess laughed. "These
are one of your magical
inventions, aren't they,
Mr Cleverfeather?"

The owl nodded.
"They're called
Super-Skates.
Try them!"

Lily and Jess did! As their feet
slipped into them, the tiny skates grew and
changed until they were a snug fit.

"Magic!" laughed Lily.

"Watch me, then I'll tell you what to do,"
Mr Cleverfeather said.

He stepped on the ice and skated forwards, backwards and in a circle.

Everyone clapped.

"Step on the ice," said Mr Cleverfeather. "Fight root first. I mean, right foot first. That's it," he added as everyone slid forwards. "Left, right…"

"These skates really are magical," Jess said. With their help, the girls were soon gliding gracefully across the frozen lake.

Lily cupped her hands around her mouth and

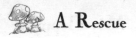

called, "Mia, we're coming!"

Mr Cleverfeather nodded. "That's right," he said. "We'll soon beach the runny."

The girls laughed so much they nearly slipped over. "He means 'reach the bunny'," Jess explained to the animals.

As they got to Mia, Lily scooped her up and cuddled her to make her warm.

"Thank you for saving me," said the bunny. "I thought I'd never get off this ice!"

Jess helped Mia put on a pair of skates. They immediately shrank to fit her little bunny paws.

Mia eagerly skated onto the ice and twirled in a graceful circle. "I can practise my pirouettes, after all!" she squealed, spinning around and around.

Goldie smiled as she watched the little bunny skating with all the other animals. "This is how happy the Frost Festival should be!" she said. "We've got to get that snowflake back. If we don't, none of these animals will get their special Frost Festival gifts!"

"Maybe our friends will help," said Lily.
"Listen, everyone," she called. "We think
the snowflake Winter Wonder has been
hidden on the lake. Will you help us to
look for it?"

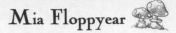

"Of course!" said the badger.

"Yes!" chorused the hamster, the vole
and the kittens.

The animals spread out to search,
skating carefully across the ice.

Barely a moment later, Jess grabbed
Lily's arm. "Oh no!" she cried, pointing.
The bears had appeared on the lake again,
and were running and sliding across the ice
towards them!

"They've spotted us!" cried Lily.

CHAPTER THREE

Icy Fun

Mr Cleverfeather gathered the animals together and stood in front of them with his wings spread.

The bears slid towards Jess and Lily.

"Hey!" cried Pearl. "You took our special sugarplum!"

"Yeah! Not fair!" said Sleet.

 93

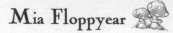

"Well, you won't find the other Wonders, so there!" Minty said, and stuck his pink tongue out at them.

"We will!" Jess called back. "There's one here somewhere, and we won't leave until we find it."

"We won't let you!" yelled Sleet. "Come on, Minty and Pearl! Let's get them!"

The bears rushed across the ice towards the girls, but Lily stepped aside and Minty skidded right past.

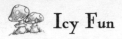

Sleet and Pearl headed straight for Mr
Cleverfeather and the animals, but they
zigzagged back and forth, dodging out
of their grasp. All three bears chased the
animals around, giggling as they slid and
rolled across the ice.

Jess, Lily, Mia and Goldie gathered
together. "Have you noticed," Jess asked,
"that even though the bears want to stop
us from searching, they're loving all the
sliding about and dodging?

They're having fun!"

"That's right," said Lily
thoughtfully.

"They loved our snowball fight yesterday, too." Jess added. "Maybe we could distract them with a game, and then we can search for the Winter Wonder without them noticing?"

"Ice hockey!" said Lily. "Let's ask Mary and Eve Redbreast if we can borrow their hockey things."

The robins happily shared out the sticks. Lily used hers to hit the puck to

Goldie, who whacked it back to Jess.

"This is fun!" Lily said loudly.

The animals all joined in, using fallen
twigs as hockey sticks.

The bears watched for a moment.
When the puck whizzed towards Pearl,
she pounced on it and slid across the ice,
shrieking with delight.

Minty chased after her and hit the puck
with his big paw.

Mia stopped it with her stick, but Sleet

swiped it away and soon all the animals

were having a happy hockey game with

the bears!

Mr Cleverfeather whispered to Lily and

Jess, "We'll keep the pears blaying –

I mean, the bears playing – while you

look for the Winter Wonder."

Goldie, Mia and the girls skated away

from the game and circled around,

searching.

"It's no good," Jess called.

"All I can see is snow!

How are we
ever going to
find *one* snowflake
in all of this?"

But as she looked around, Lily spotted
something. One snowflake wasn't
floating down to the icy lake, but
hanging in the air!
Could it be?
"Look, Jess!"
Lily cried, skating
towards it. "I think
it's the snowflake!"

Holding hands, Jess and Lily skated over, but as they did there was a sharp crack.

Lily glanced down and saw the ice under her skates splitting into pieces. "Oh no!" she cried. "The ice – it's breaking!"

CHAPTER FOUR

Brave Bunny

The two girls skated over to the safety of the lake's edge. "We must find a way to reach the snowflake," said Jess. "I know! Maybe the birds could fly to it. Mary! Eve! Mr Cleverfeather!"

The three birds broke away from the hockey game and skated toward them.

Lily explained the problem, asking, "Could you fly over the thin ice in the middle of the lake and pick up the snowflake?"

Mary and Eve tried to flap their snow-dusted wings. But they couldn't even take off! "Our feathers are weighed down," said Eve.

"The snow's too heavy for my old wings, too," said Mr Cleverfeather. "It's like wearing a chilly coat."

"It's up to us, then," Jess said.

The girls tried lying on their tummies

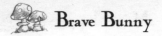

and using swimming movements to scoot
along. But when they reached the thin
ice, it creaked.

"Come back!" Goldie cried in alarm.
"Thin ice is dangerous!"

The girls scooted back to where the ice
was thicker.

"If only there was a way to cross that
thin ice," Jess said with a sigh.

"There is!" cried Mia.

The girls stared at her.

"When I do my dance," she said, "I
have to pirouette on tippy toes." Mia's
eyes shone. "I'll tippytoe across the ice.

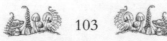

I'm so little and light, it won't break!"

Jess and Lily both felt anxious. "What if you fall through?" Jess asked.

"I won't!" Mia said. "Let me try – it's the only way to get the snowflake."

Goldie glanced at the girls. They all nodded.

"Mia, you hold one end of my scarf," said Goldie. "I'll hold the other end. Then if you do fall in, we can pull you straight back out."

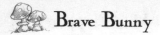

Mia took a deep breath and slowly,
slowly, tippytoed lightly across the ice.

"It's almost as if she's floating," said
Jess. "And Goldie's scarf is
growing longer and longer –
it's magical!"

"Mia's nearly there," Lily
said. "Just a little further..."

Goldie's ears pricked up.
"What's that?"

Before the girls could reply, they heard
a terrible sound, "Graaarr!"

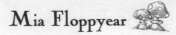

Lily clutched Goldie's paw, and turned
to see the three bears skating towards
them, looking very annoyed.

"Stop those girls!" Minty yelled.

"They've found the Wonder!"

Jess called to Mia, "Hurry!"

The brave bunny ran a few more steps

 106

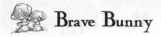
toward the middle of the lake, leaped like
a ballerina into the air, and grabbed the
snowflake. "I've got it!" she cried.

Goldie pulled the scarf and Mia slid
back to the safety of the thicker ice.
She skated to the girls, clutching the
shimmering snowflake in her tiny paws.

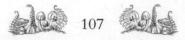

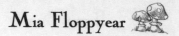

"Hooray!" cried Jess, picking Mia up and giving her a hug. "We've got the second Wonder!"

CHAPTER FIVE

Presents!

The bears slid across the ice, but Goldie and the girls were faster thanks to their Super-Skates. They reached the shore and looked back.

To their surprise, the three bears had stopped chasing them.

"They've given up," Jess said, surprised.

"They're yawning again," Lily giggled.

"We've still got one Wonder!" Pearl shouted sleepily. "And it's the best of all, because it makes everything snowy!"

"That's right!" Sleet continued. "And we've hidden it where you'll never get it!"

All three bears linked arms and trudged away across the ice, yawning noisily.

"Phew!" said Lily. "It's lucky they keep getting sleepy. I wonder why?"

"Maybe it's because they're young," Jess said. "Come on, let's put the snowflake back where it belongs. Then everyone will get their special winter gifts!"

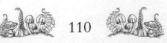

Jess, Lily, Goldie and Mia thanked all the animals for their help.

"And thank you, especially, Mr Cleverfeather," Lily added, as they piled their skates back on his sledge. She giggled as the skates wriggled and shrank until they were all the same paw shape.

"Mia!" a voice called.

Jess and Lily turned. It was Mia's dad, Mr Floppyear.

"Dad!" Mia cried. "We had an adventure and I helped and I was brave and I got the snowflake Winter Wonder for Jess and Lily!"

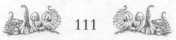

"I'm very proud of you," said Mr Floppyear, "but it's home time now."

Goldie nodded. "It's late," she said. "Lily and Jess, would you like another sleepover in my Grotto? Tomorrow we could search for the third Winter Wonder together."

"We'd love to!" Lily said.

"Me, too! Me, too!" cried Mia. "Dad! Dad! Can I? Can I go on the sleepover, too? Pleeeease?"

Mr Floppyear looked at Goldie,

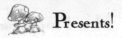

Presents!

who smiled and nodded. His whiskers twitched. "All right, Mia," he said.

"We'll look after her," Jess promised. "Goodbye, everyone. See you tomorrow."

All the animals called, "Goodbye!" except Mr Cleverfeather, who said, "Bye Jess! Lie Billy! I mean, Bye Lily!"

The girls were still giggling as they carried the snowflake back to its icy pedestal.

This time, Jess lifted Mia up and she carefully put the snowflake back. It sent out tiny silver sparkles that glittered in the falling snow.

113

As they walked back to Goldie's
Grotto, brightly wrapped gifts magically
appeared outside each little cottage and
den. There were squeals of delight from
the Twinkletails' cottage.

"Presents!" the little mice squeaked.

The girls heard more excited cries
echoing through the trees.

"I've got a present!" croaked one of the
Greenhop frogs.

Goldie smiled happily. "The snowflake's
magic is working already!"

As they reached Goldie's Grotto, Lily
peered through the falling snow.

 114

"There's something on your doorstep, Goldie," she said.

Jess ran to see. "Presents!" she cried. "Four of them — one for each of us!"

Mia picked hers up and shook it. "Ooh! What's this?"

"Let's get comfortable before we open them," suggested Goldie.

Soon they were settled among plump cushions, drinking steaming hot chocolate.

Mia unwrapped her gift. She opened it and found a bracelet with a tiny silver ballet dancer charm on it.

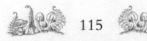

"Ooh, I love it," she said. "I hope I can wear it to the Winter Dance! What have you got, Goldie?"

"Let's see," said Goldie, opening her gift. "It's a hot-water bottle! Perfect for snowy weather." She looked closer. "I do believe it's magical," she said. "Look."

It was deep blue, with a gold rose on the front and words beneath.

Goldie smiled. "It says,

If you want cosy toes

Press my golden rose."

She pressed it, and then gasped. "It's warm already!"

"Wow!" said Jess. "That's amazing!"

Inside Lily's parcel was a little box of four chocolates, all decorated with pretty violet icing swirls.

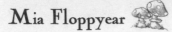

"Let's share!" Lily said, and they all took one each.

"Mmm, that was yummy," said Mia. "It's a shame there aren't any more."

Lily gasped. "But there are!" she said. "Have another one, everybody."

They did, and Goldie laughed at Lily's look of surprise as the box was magically filled again. "It's because you were generous, and shared them," she said. "What have you got, Jess?"

"EverSharp Colouring Pencils," said Jess. "Fantastic! I desperately need new ones. My old ones are worn to stumps."

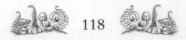

She looked round. "You can borrow them whenever you like."

"Let's get some rest," said Goldie. "We've got a difficult search tomorrow."

They snuggled down among the cushions and cosy blankets.

"There's still one more Winter Wonder to find," said Jess, "and if we don't…"

"I won't get to dance at the Winter Dance!" Mia said.

And Grizelda will have Friendship Forest for herself," Lily finished. "We've got to stop her!"

Story Three
Snowdrop

CHAPTER ONE

Captain Ace's News

The next morning, Jess, Lily and Mia
woke up and ate chocolate pancakes as
fast as Goldie could make them.

Lily looked through the window at the
huge piles of snow outside. "We've still
got to find the third Winter Wonder," she
said. "But how will we ever find a small

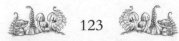

white flower in all this snow?"

"It'll be hard," said Goldie, "but we have to do it, or we can't stop Grizelda's witchy winter plan."

"How can that horrid witch be so mean?" Mia burst out.

"Come on." Jess jumped up. "Let's get going!" She passed round the magical hats and scarves the Woollyhop family had given them. It was so cold that even Mia was getting chilly, so Lily tucked the bunny into her coat, while Goldie pressed the golden rose on her hot water bottle and gave it to Mia to cuddle.

"It's hard to see," said Jess, as the snow came down all around them. "Stay together, so we don't get lost."

As they crossed a clearing, leaving deep footprints, they heard wings flapping and down flew Captain Ace the stork.

"Terrible, terrible," he said, shaking his head. "I'm the only bird big and strong enough to fly in such snow. I came to tell you that I've just flown over Harmony Hall, and it's icier than ever."

"Oh no!" wailed Mia. "But the Winter Dance is supposed to be today! It will definitely be cancelled now."

"Maybe not," Captain Ace said kindly. "I spotted something else. The three white bears who took the Winter Wonders are on the Honeysuckle Hills, beyond Sunshine Meadow." He frowned, "they were digging in the snow."

"Maybe they were hiding the snowdrop?" said Goldie. "Thanks, Captain Ace!"

Lily nodded. "Let's chase after them! Oh, but it'll take ages to get there through all this snow."

Jess had a brainwave. "Yesterday Mr Cleverfeather used a sledge to carry his Super-Skates. Let's ask if we can borrow it to ride on. We can pull it uphill, then all get on and whizz downhill."

"Brilliant!" said Lily. "That will save lots of time!"

They headed for the tree where Mr

127

Cleverfeather had his inventing shed.
Captain Ace walked alongside, sheltering
them from the snow under his wings.

But Mr Cleverfeather wasn't in his shed.
He was working outside on the ground,
putting the finishing touches to a shiny
red sleigh.

"Wow!" cried Mia. "That's beautiful!"

Jess looked at Lily, her eyes sparkling.
"A sleigh would be even quicker than
a sledge!" she said, with a grin.

CHAPTER TWO

Honeysuckle Hills

"Of course you can take my sleigh to Sunny Huckle Hills," Mr Cleverfeather said, patting the shiny new invention. "I mean—"

Everyone laughed.

"We know what you mean," said Lily. "And thank you."

The old owl put a wingtip to his forehead and thought for a moment. Then he said, "I've got some even more useful things you can borrow." He flew to his shed in the treetop and, moments later, lowered down a huge basket on a rope.

Jess and Lily steadied it as it reached the ground.

Mr Cleverfeather flew down and began pulling things out of the basket.

"Skis for you all," he said, loading them into a box at the back of the sleigh. "And a tiny blue sledge for a tiny rabbit," he added, winking at Mia.

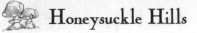

She clapped her paws in delight.

Mr Cleverfeather stacked more things into the box. "There! Rude, bugs and a funny blanket." He shook his head. "I mean food, rugs and a bunny blanket!"

Mia jumped on the sleigh, clutching the hot-water bottle, as the owl tucked the blanket around her.

Jess and Lily were puzzled.

"The sleigh's great," said Lily, "but who will pull it?"

Mr Cleverfeather smiled. "I've already invited someone to try it out in all this snow. She'll be here any minute."

He'd barely finished speaking when a grey and white Shetland pony trotted through the trees.

"This is Mrs Dappletrot," said Mr Cleverfeather. He introduced Goldie, Mia and the girls.

"Hello! I've heard how much Jess and Lily have done for our forest," said the

pony. "If I can do anything for you, I'd be glad."

Lily explained about chasing the bears.

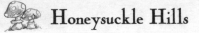

"Would you be kind enough to pull the sleigh to Honeysuckle Hills?" she asked.

Mr Cleverfeather laughed. "Mrs Dappletrot only needs to guide the sleigh, not pull it," he said. "All aboard!"

Goldie and the girls climbed on the sleigh with Mia, while Mrs Dappletrot fitted its strong leather straps over her shoulders.

Mr Cleverfeather pressed a green button on the side of the sleigh. With a gurgling, burbling sound, bubbles appeared from underneath. Then more bubbles, and more!

The sleigh wobbled slightly,
and lifted off the ground.

"Bubble power!" cried Jess. "The sleigh
floats on bubble power, just like your
balloon, Captain Ace!"

"Ready?" asked Mrs Dappletrot.

"Ready!" said Lily. "Goodbye Mr
Cleverfeather, goodbye Captain Ace!"

The little pony trotted through the trees,
with the sleigh floating behind her.

"This is amazing!" cried Jess.

As Mrs Dappletrot broke into a canter, the sleigh skimmed the snow, swooping and swaying from side to side.

"Wheee!" cried Mia.

They zoomed across Sunshine Meadow, then through more trees. When they emerged, the snow-covered Honeysuckle Hills lay before them, looking like giant white pillows. The pony pulled them up and down the hills, and the girls squealed in delight. "It's just like a snowy rollercoaster ride!" Jess said.

As they got to the top of the highest

hill, Mia pointed and cried, "Something

moved down there!"

"It must be the bears," said Lily.

"We'll ski from here so they don't see

us. Thank you, Mrs Dappletrot!"

When Goldie and the girls

put their feet on the skis,

little straps magically

appeared around

their boots.

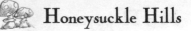

Mia climbed up on the little blue sledge.

"Good luck!" said Mrs Dappletrot, as they set off.

They skied down the steep slope, trying to stay quiet, but Mia's sledge slid so fast that it shot past Goldie, Lily and Jess, heading straight towards the bears!

Lily and Jess sped after her, but it was too late! Mia's sledge turned sideways and tipped over and Mia tumbled into the snow, crying out in surprise.

The bears looked up towards her.

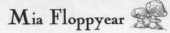

Jess picked Mia up, while Lily watched the bears anxiously.

"You're too late!" Pearl called. "We've hidden the Wonder on these hills. You'll never, ever find a little snowdrop in all this snow!"

Lily and Jess looked at each other sadly. What were they going to do?

CHAPTER THREE

Avalanche!

Jess and Lily watched as the bears climbed to the top of the neighbouring hill and huddled together.

"Captain Ace said that they were burying something this morning," Lily remembered. "Maybe we can spot where the snow has been disturbed?"

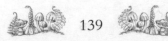

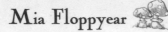

"Look! The snow looks untidy there."
Mia pointed a paw down near where the
bears had just been standing.

Goldie, Jess and Lily skied down to
the bottom of the hill, with Mia sledding
behind them.

At the bottom of the hill the snow was
all messy and lumpy and covered with
bear pawprints.

"Someone's definitely been digging
here," Goldie said happily.

"Then we should search here! I'm a
good digger," Mia said. "Watch!" She
bent down and set to work, her fluffy tail

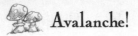

bobbing as she flung snow into the air.

"I know how to clear snow quickly,"
said Jess. "Snow angels!"

"What are those?" asked Goldie.

"We'll show you," said Lily.

She and Jess lay on their backs, and
moved their arms up and down, making
angel wings in the snow. Then they moved
their legs from side to side to make the
angel dress.

"That looks fun!" said Mia. "I'll make a bunny angel!"

They all made angels – lots of them – but there was still just too much snow.

"This isn't working," Jess said sadly. "We must try something else if we're going to save Friendship Forest."

Goldie shivered. "Prrrr! It's cold."

"Ooh! Ooh!" cried Mia, hopping up and down and swishing snow off of her pink tutu. "Your hot-water bottle!"

She fetched it and pressed the golden rose. Everyone put their hands and paws on the bottle.

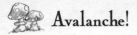

"That's lovely," said Jess. "Let's take turns cuddling it until our hands are warm!"

"I've got an idea," Lily said slowly. "Let's put the hot-water bottle on the ground, and drag it along so it melts the snow, just like the hotpots melted the entrance to the Tippytoes studio. Maybe it will uncover the snowdrop!"

"Great idea!" said Jess.

They took turns sweeping the hot water bottle through the snow. Some of the snow melted, making little puddles, but it still wasn't enough.

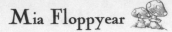

"At this rate, the snow will be up to the treetops before we find the snowdrop," Jess said, gloomily.

Mia gave a shout. "Look! Up there! What's happening?"

The three white bears stood at the top of the hill beside three gigantic snowballs.

"Go!" shouted Pearl.

The huge snowballs rolled downhill towards the watching friends, slowly at first, then faster and faster. On the way down they gathered more and more snow, growing bigger and scarier.

"It's an avalanche!" Jess yelled. "Run!"

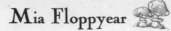

It was too late. The huge snowballs crashed into them and smothered the four friends in thick snow!

CHAPTER FOUR

A Magical Dance

As Jess struggled to free herself from the snowfall, she heard the bears giggling.

"Wasn't that fun?" said Sleet's voice.

"It'll stop them finding the Winter Wonder," laughed Minty.

Jess's hands and arms broke free. She cleared snow from her face and found

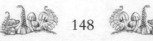

Lily and Goldie doing the same.

"Where's Mia?" Lily cried.

A cross squeaking sound came

from a huge heap

of snow. The

edge of a

pink tutu

appeared,

followed by a fluffy

bunny tail. Mia burst out backwards and

plopped down with a gasp.

They all hugged and huddled together.

Everyone was cold and wet and shivery.

They found the hot-water bottle, but its

148

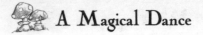

magical heat couldn't possibly warm all of them.

Goldie looked around desperately. "We'll never find that snowdrop," she said. "There's just too much snow."

"We must be in the right area," Lily insisted. "Otherwise the bears wouldn't be trying to stop us. We must have missed it somehow — let's look again."

Jess shivered. "We need to warm ourselves up first."

"Let's dance!" said Mia, putting the hot water bottle down. "Dancing will warm us up. Copy me and we'll soon be toasty.

Ready? Jump, jump, jump!"

They jumped.

"Hop, hop, hop!" said Mia.

Everybody hopped.

"Jump, hop, jump, hop!"

This time, everyone got muddled, and they burst out laughing.

"I feel warmer," said Goldie. "Dancing's definitely good for cold weather!"

Mia stopped suddenly. "Ooh! Ooh!" she cried. "Why don't we try Wendy Inkwing's Snow-Away Dance again? Maybe it'll work and melt the snow. Then we'll see the snowdrop!"

150

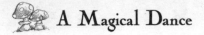

"We could try," Goldie said doubtfully.

Lily wasn't sure either. "If it didn't work before, Mia, it won't work now."

Mia wriggled with excitement. "I remember the steps," she said. "I'll show you, but we must dance harder this time." She began the rhyme.

"Dance in a circle around and around…"

Everyone turned around in a circle.

"Reach to the sky and then reach to the ground."

They stretched up, down, then did it once more.

"Clap paws together, up high, down low…"

They clapped as high as they could, then down by their knees.

"Now you will see the cold snow GO!"

Nothing happened. Everyone was so disappointed, but little Mia insisted on trying again.

"Dance even harder," she said.

Off they went again. But this time, when Mia said, "Clap paws together," she tripped over the hot-water bottle.

Jess and Lily rushed to stop her falling. Each caught hold of one of her paws.

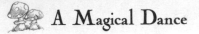

Lily stood for a moment. Holding Mia's paw gave her an idea. "Maybe we've been getting the steps wrong," she said. "Let's do it differently. Instead of dancing in our own little circle, let's hold hands – and paws – and dance in a circle together!"

"Of course!" said Jess. "And when we have to clap paws – and hands – together, let's clap with whoever's next to us!"

Mia chanted the words again. This time, they danced together, instead of alone. "Now you will see the cold snow GO!" Mia finished.

All around them, the snow on the trees began to melt and drip off. Goldie gave a shout. "It's working!" she cried.

Lily was thrilled. "Dance again!" she called to the others.

This time, when Mia said, "Now you

will see the cold snow GO!" the friends held their breath. To their delight, the snow all around melted more and more.

"Look, the grass is showing through!" cried Goldie, pointing her paw at a snowy puddle.

"And flowers," said Jess, as a tangle of honeysuckle was revealed at her feet.

Lily shrieked with joy. There, in the melting snow, was a tiny, delicate flower. "The snowdrop!"

The third Winter Wonder was nestling among glossy green leaves in a little dip in the hillside. Lily ran to fetch it.

She held it up for everyone to see. Its white petals opened, revealing smaller petals inside, tipped with sparkling green.

"Hooray!" they cried. "We've found it!"

CHAPTER FIVE

Harmony Hall

Lily and Jess looked at the magical snowdrop in delight.

"We just need to put it back on the pedestal, and the snow will go back to normal," Goldie said happily.

"And we can have the Winter Dance after all!" Mia twirled.

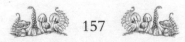

Just then there was a "grrrr!" from the hilltop. The bears had spotted that they had the snowdrop!

"Oh no! We've lost all the Winter Wonders!" said Minty.

Sleet clutched Pearl's arm. "Grizelda's going to be cross," he said.

"We ought to run away," Pearl said, yawning, "but I'm too tired."

The bears curled up together on the ground. Jess walked up to them. "Why are you so sleepy?" she asked gently.

"We should be hibernating," said Minty. "Grizelda woke us up and promised we'd get lots of snowy fun if we helped her."

Now Jess and Lily understood. The bears needed to sleep through the winter!

"Can't you go back to Snowcap Mountain?" asked Goldie.

Pearl shook her head. "It's too far for tired bears," she said.

"You could sleep in your igloo," suggested Mia, "but I suppose it will soon melt now that we've found the snowdrop."

No one knew what to do. The bears were almost nodding off.

Jess had a thought. "Remember our adventures with Sophie Flufftail the

squirrel and Chilly the ice dragon?"

Lily and Goldie nodded.

Jess turned to the bears. "We know a magical place called the Winter Cave," she explained. "It's nice and cold all the time! You could sleep there until you're ready to go home."

"But if we let you use it, you must promise to leave the Winter Wonders alone," Lily said.

"We will! We will!" cried the bears.

They headed through the falling snow back to the sleigh, where Mrs Dappletrot was waiting patiently, her warm breath

making clouds in the chilly air. Then
everyone piled in, cuddling together as
the bubbles worked their magic. Lily
grinned as she huddled next to the bear
cubs. Minty, Sleet and Pearl might be
naughty, but their fur was so soft!

Mrs Dappletrot knew where the Winter
Cave was and took them straight there.

Mia waited in the sleigh as Lily showed
the bears their new winter home. Goldie
and Jess followed with blankets and food
from the back of the sleigh. Soon the
bears were cuddled sleepily together.

Jess laid more soft covers over them and

tucked them in, making sure they were cosy, snuggly and warm.

"Thank you," Sleet murmured.

"Sorry about the Wonders," said Pearl.

"Goodnight," yawned Minty.

They fell asleep, making snuffly snoring sounds in their snug nest of blankets.

Lily dropped a goodnight kiss on each white furry head.

"Sweet dreams," Jess whispered, as they left the cave.

Mrs Dappletrot led the sleigh back to the clearing, and Lily hurried to put the snowdrop back on its ice pedestal. Right away, pale green and white sparkles showered down on the snow below. To everyone's delight, snow stopped falling, and the deep snowdrifts began to melt. In minutes, the forest went back to normal, with just a pretty sprinkling of snow.

"That's exactly how it was when we arrived!" said Lily.

Jess, Lily, Mia and Goldie clasped hands and paws and danced around. "Hooray! We've saved the Frost Festival!"

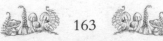

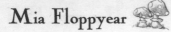

Mia led them in a celebration dance, then Jess stopped and groaned. "Oh, no!"

A yellow-green orb of light floated towards them and exploded in a shower of stinking sparks.

"Go away, Grizelda!" Jess shouted.

Then she jumped back in fright as the witch appeared, screeching at the top of her voice. "You horrible, interfering girls! You and that cat and that dancing rabbit have ruined my witchy winter and made me lose my bears! But never fear, I'll be back to take over the forest – and soon!"

Her green hair whipped and crackled

 164

around her head nastily.

"So watch out!" the witch screamed.
"You haven't seen the last of Grizelda!"

She snapped her fingers and
disappeared in another shower of sparks.

"She's gone," Lily said in relief.

"Hooray!" cheered Mia, spinning round
and round on her tiptoes. "Now we can
have the Winter Dance!"

Jess, Lily and Goldie sat on a glistening
pink rock bench in Harmony Hall. The
whole of the theatre was made of the

same pretty pink stone. All around them, the snow sparkled beautifully in the sun.

The theatre was packed. It seemed as if every animal in Friendship Forest was there. Lots of the girls' friends came over to hug them.

"Thank you for saving our forest from freezing!" said Grace Woollyhop.

"Thank you for stopping Grizelda's wicked plan!" said Emily Prickleback.

The show opened with Wendy Inkwing and the Tippytoes dancers in a ballet called Frost Flowers. All the dancers wore

lovely flower garlands on their heads!
Then came the Fuzzybrush fox family,
who danced their beautiful star dance.

Then Mr Cleverfeather came on stage
with a red top hat, a walking cane and
shiny red shoes. He did a tap dance,
and whenever he dropped the cane it
magically sprang back to his wingtip.

Finally, it was time for Mia's big solo.
The little rabbit leaped onto the stage in
her pink tutu, and everybody cheered!
Her face was filled with joy as she danced
gracefully, performing perfect pirouettes.

The watching animals had heard how Mia had helped defeat Grizelda. When she finished with an elegant curtsey, everyone stood up and clapped and cheered the brave little bunny.

"Hooray for Mia!" cried Lily and Jess.

All the dancers came on stage for a final bow. Goldie and the girls presented posies to the dancers, with especially big ones for Wendy Inkwing and Mia.

Soon it was time for everyone to go home. Mia jumped lightly from the stage to hug the girls.

"You have to come back and watch my next dance!" she said.

Jess smiled. "We will."

They followed Goldie to the Friendship Tree. She touched the trunk and opened the door that appeared. Golden light shone out.

"Thank you for saving the forest, and the Frost Festival," she said.

"If Grizelda starts plotting again, just come for us," said Lily. "We'll be ready."

Goldie hugged them, then Lily followed Jess into the golden light. They felt the

tingle that meant they were growing back to their proper size.

When they emerged, they found it was still snowing in Brightley.

"What an amazing snowy adventure," said Lily. Holding hands, she and Jess danced through the snowflakes back to the wildlife hospital.

"Let's go and make sure the animals are cosy," said Jess.

Lily laughed. "Just like the three bears!"

The End

Grizelda has cast a spell on the Memory Tree, and now the animals are forgetting everything! Can Jess, Lily and little bear cub Hannah Honeypaw help their friends to remember?

Find out in the next adventure,

Hannah Honeypaw's Forgetful Day

Turn over for a sneak peek ...

Lily and Jess stared in horror as the lights flew into the clearing.

Behind Grizelda's familiar yellow-green orb bobbed four others – one purple, one blue, one green and one bright yellow. The biggest orb burst into a shower of smelly sparks. It was Grizelda the wicked witch!

Grizelda was wearing a purple tunic over black trousers and high-heeled boots. Her green hair swirled wildly around her head, like squabbling snakes.

"Ha! It's the interfering girls and their cat," she sneered. "And a silly bear!"

Hannah Honeypaw shrank back behind the girls.

"Leave her alone, Grizelda!" shouted Jess. "She's only little."

"I've got some little friends, too," Grizelda said, and snapped her fingers.

The four smaller orbs burst into showers of sparks. In their places stood four small witches!

Read

Hannah Honeypaw's Forgetful Day

to find out what happens next!

Magic
Animal Friends

Look out for the brand-new
Magic Animal Friends series,
coming soon!

Series Four

www.magicanimalfriends.com